STEP BROTHER
with Benefits

SECOND SEASON

MIA CLARK

Copyright © 2015 Mia Clark

All rights reserved.

ISBN: 1517227194
ISBN-13: 978-1517227197

Book design by Cerys du Lys
Cover design by Cerys du Lys
Cover Image © Depositphotos | avgustino

Cherrylily.com

DEDICATION

Thank you to Ethan and Cerys for helping me with this book and everything involved in the process. This is a dream come true and I wouldn't have been able to do it without them. Thank you, thank you!

CONTENTS

ACKNOWLEDGMENTS

Thank you for taking a chance on my book!

I know that the stepbrother theme can be a difficult one to deal with for a lot of people for a variety of reasons, and so I took that into consideration when I was writing this. While this is a story about forbidden love, it's also a story about two people becoming friends, too. Sometimes you need someone to push you in your life, even when you think everything is fine. Sometimes you need someone to be there, even when you don't know how to ask them to stay with you.

This is that kind of story. It is about two people becoming friends, and then becoming lovers. The forbidden aspects add tension, but it's more than that, too. Sometimes opposites attract in the best way possible. I hope you enjoy my books!

STEPBROTHER WITH BENEFITS

Introduction

OW DID I WIND UP NAKED, body tensing in orgasm on the pool table (not my first orgasm, just so you know), my stepbrother thrusting hard into me, calling me his dirty princess, while both of us were so lost in lust that we barely realized our parents were calling our names? Well, that's kind of a long story. I don't know how I keep ending up in situations like this. It never seemed to happen to me before my accidental one night stand with Ethan about a week ago, but it's becoming increasingly more common.

I don't even know if I can call myself a good girl anymore, because good girls definitely don't do things like this. They don't let their stepbrothers coax them into stripping down in the game room, they don't willingly agree to lay down on the pool table naked, and they wouldn't let him use some sort of crazy vibrator on them, but Ethan and I just did that, too. And good girls definitely don't ignore the fact that they knew their mother and stepfather were coming home today--any minute now, too--but they thought it'd be fine to give in to a little fun and games, because...

Because why? I have no idea! This isn't my fault. It's Ethan's. He's the bad boy in this relationship.

Relationship? Um... yes... did I mention we're dating now? Because we are.

Maybe I should backtrack a little and start over from the beginning. Not too far, just a little bit. It's easier to explain that way.

"Ashley! Are you here--?"

I barely hear my mom's voice, because Ethan's in my ear at the same time.

"Are you?" he asks.

I nod at him and bite my bottom lip, concentrating on the feeling of him inside me, filling me, of him luring me into temptation and ecstasy.

"Ethan, I... I'm cumming," I tell him. "Now. Right now."

Yes, well, um...

1 – Ashley

(About an hour earlier)

E THAN!" I PROTEST. "They're going to be back soon."

"Who?" he asks, feigning ignorance. He knows exactly who I mean!

"Um, my mom? Your dad? Hello? They're coming back today. Business trip, remember?"

"Fuck," he says, but he doesn't even sound genuinely annoyed. He's smirking at me with that bad boy grin of his, and he won't stop touching me.

I don't want him to stop touching me either, though. I love the feeling of his hands on my hips, caressing upwards, towards... um, well, right now I'm wearing a bathing suit, because we just got out of the pool. It's sort of strange because we've gone swimming every day for the past few days, but we haven't worn bathing suits. It's just swimming! We, um... alright, so we had sex in the pool a few times, but I didn't mean to!

I'm really bad at being a good girl, aren't I? I blame Ethan. He's corrupting me. It's the perfect excuse, but I'm not sure how much longer I can keep using it.

"Listen, Princess," he says. "I know they're going to be back soon, but that just means we've got to make the best of this while we still can, right?"

I give him a dirty look, but dirty looks don't work on him, apparently. Or, they work but he just takes it as a flirty glance instead of me trying to get him to realize this is a bad idea. Bad boys love bad ideas, though. It's kind of their thing, isn't it? Ethan's no exception.

I change tact, trying to convince him that um... well, I do try to slap his hands away from my hips, but he just grabs me even harder, pulling me against him. I can feel the press of his erection through his swimsuit, and it's pushed right against my crotch. Ethan sways side to side, pulling me closer to him, as close as he can, rubbing his cock against my bikini bottom-covered pussy.

What am I even supposed to say to that? I don't know! I'm not used to this. I kind of want to get used to it, but... not now! Our parents! They'll be back um... I glance over to the clock on the wall, and it looks like we do have a little time left. Maybe...

This is a very bad idea. Very very bad. Very very very very bad, and I'm about to agree to it. No, I do. I did. Maybe. Almost. He's basically already convinced me, but I'm trying to convince him not to convince me. How does that even work? Ugh!

"You're still my stepbrother, you know?" I tell him. "It doesn't matter that you've tricked my mom into letting you date me, because I don't think our parents are going to be too happy about finding you actively seducing me in the middle of the living room."

"Nah," he says, grinning. "I wasn't planning on staying in the living room."

"The bedroom would be a lot more appropriate," I tell him, nodding. "It's harder for them to um... complain... no, actually, Ethan, I know we're trying to do this. This um... relationship thing, right?"

"Yeah," he says. "What about it?"

"I just... I think maybe we shouldn't have sex, though. I mean, not with our parents around. That's kind of weird."

"What the fuck, why?" he asks.

He sounds distraught and confused, which is kind of funny. I don't mean to, but I start to laugh.

"Wow, you're laughing when we're trying to have a serious conversation? My own stepsister is mocking me. I can't believe this."

"You're so gross!" I tell him, making a face at him and sticking out my tongue.

Unfortunately this is a bad idea, because he just grins and licks the tip of my tongue, before licking even further, and then before I know it we're kissing. My tongue teases and dances with his, and I almost lose track of myself, my body, our situation. His hands fumble with the ties of my bikini top. I don't even usually wear bikinis, but Ethan insisted. He makes me feel so sexy, even when I never thought I was before.

It's weird because I've seen him this way before. Sometimes I worry and wonder about it. Is this real? Ethan's got a reputation for "dating" girls for a week or two, if you can even call it that. He says he's never dated anyone, but he's certainly gone out with them, had sex with them, done his bad boy thing with them, and then stopped talking to them, stopped texting them, no more calls, no more contact except for the occasional booty call.

This is different, though. He's said things like this to other girls, and he's done things like this, too. I never saw the full extent of it, but I know he's done it. I think he really means it this time, though. With... with me. We've been through a lot, and done so much, and... I don't know... I'm lost in the moment and I desperately want it to be real.

I push him away before he can figure out how to untie my bikini top, and I stare hard at him. I put my hands on my hips and try to look serious and indignant, but I'm nervous.

"Ethan, um... tell me the truth! Do you want to date me? Is this real? You're not just um... you know? You're not, are you?"

"Ashley, cut it out," he says. "No, I'm not. I want to date you. You don't even fucking know how much I want to date you. Is this about the sex stuff? I can ease up if you really need me to, but seriously I want to fuck the shit out of you right now, you don't even know. I have no idea why the sight of you in that bikini makes me so hard. I've seen you naked so many times, but this is different. Fuck! You're so sexy, Princess."

I wasn't expecting that. I blush and look away, but Ethan closes the distance between us and pulls me back, his fingers grabbing my chin, making me look at him.

"Seriously," he says. "You're sexy as fuck, but it's more, too. I've never felt this way about anyone before. I want to date you. I want to have a real relationship with you. If I'm being real fucking honest, right now I want to fuck you hard, though. If you want me to stop, I can stop. I'll do it for you."

"I don't want you to stop," I say, half whining and half begging. What am I even begging for? Um... I know exactly what, but I don't want to admit it. "Our parents are going to be home soon, though! We can't just... we can't just do this! Not right here?"

"Yeah, fuck, of course not. I know we can't do it right here," he says, smiling. He takes my hand in his, squeezing it tight and leading me away. "Why the fuck would we have sex in the living room when we can do it in the game room on the pool table. I've got a surprise for you, too. Kind of want to test it out, if you're up for it. I promise you'll love it."

I love the way he squeezes my hand and leads me along, keeping me close, never letting me go. I'm also pretty sure he's joking about the game room, right? It's a joke and he's going to bring me to the stairs and we'll go up to either his bedroom or mine, and then...

No, he really does lead me to the game room, with the pool table sitting right in the center.

"What! You're serious?" I ask. "I thought you were joking."

"I don't make jokes, Princess. Having sex with you is the most serious thing I can think of. It's no laughing matter."

He says this, but then why is he grinning at me like an idiot. Probably because he is one! I'm the smart one, I guess. The good girl who is supposed to balance out Ethan's bad boy ways, except this isn't even how it works. I don't balance anything, I just get trapped in his... his schemes!

I tell him this, too. "I'm not going to get trapped in your bad boy schemes anymore!"

"Can you just make this easier for the both of us and take off your bikini now?" he asks.

"No!" I shout, crossing my hands over my chest. Or kind of under my chest, which I belatedly realize props up my breasts, attracting Ethan's gaze. He stares openly, grinning even more now. "Stop looking at me like a piece of meat, Ethan!" I yell at him. This is supposed to be tough and fierce, but I think I squeak partway through.

"Nah," he says. "I'm just admiring the art of your femininity. You've got classic beauty, curves in all the right places, and I want to map out your existence with my fingers like an artist painting his masterpiece on a blank canvas."

That sounds wonderful and romantic, which is exactly how I know he read this exact line somewhere. "What book did you read that from?" I ask. "I can't believe you're reading. Didn't you make fun of me a week ago by asking if I was just going to sit home alone all summer and do book reports?"

"Fuck, I thought it was romantic," he says. "How'd you know?"

"That's exactly how I knew! Because it sounds romantic."

"Fuck!" he says again, not even hiding the fact that he doesn't care, that it doesn't bother him in the least that I've called him out on his bad boy shenanigans. "Look, can you just get naked now?"

"I'm not getting--" I start to tell him off, but he just walks away. He walks away! How rude. "What are you doing?" I ask.

He goes to the closet in the game room and pulls some wand or something off a shelf there. It looks kind of like some medieval weapon, I guess? It's a white, medium-sized stick, about the length of my forearm, with a ball on one end, and a cord to plug it into the wall on the other end. I guess they didn't have cords or electricity in medieval times, but the rest of it reminds me of some knight's weapon. Ethan Colton is definitely not a chivalrous knight, though.

"Get naked and I'll show you," he says.

"Our parents are going to be home soon!" I whine at him.

"You better get naked fast then, don't you think?" he counters. Oh, Ethan, always the voice of reason.

How do you even reason with a bad boy? If you know of a good way, please tell me, because I certainly haven't figured it out yet.

I don't know why I'm doing this, except that the way he looks at me, the grin fit to split his face, ear to ear, when I tuck my fingers into the waistband of my bikini bottoms and slowly slip them down my thighs... I don't know if I should be saying this, but it turns me on a lot. I love the way he looks at me, and I love how I have some power over him like that. Yes, Ethan's a bad boy, but I'm learning a little more about his bad boy ways every day. He might be rough and rude and vulgar and more than a bit obscene, but the fact that he stops everything to stare at me like this when I... well, you know?

I peel my partly wet bathing suit down my thighs, leaving a trail of slick wetness in its wake. I'm going to pretend that the wetness between my legs is entirely from us having been in the pool a few minutes earlier, but it's probably not. Actually, I know it's not. Um... alright, so as much as I was protesting, I'm definitely interested in seeing what Ethan has in mind. I let my bikini bottoms pool at my feet, leaving my lower body completely bare for him. He comes over and places the electric wand thing on the pool table, then reaches out and cups my sex, claiming me as his.

"Ethan, I..."

Quick, not letting me think, making me live in the moment, he slips a finger inside of my slick folds, then crushes his lips to mine, kissing me.

"Fuck, you're beautiful," he whispers into my mouth. "I love you."

"I love you, too," I say, smiling, giddy. Hearing him say that, and saying it back to him, sends a shivering trill through my body. It's so exciting! Exciting, and...

"Now get this fucking top off and lay on the pool table," he says, pulling the ties of my bikini top.

The front, my cups, fall loose, barely even bothering to cover my breasts anymore. I screech and grab at them, holding them close to my body.

"Wow!" I say, rolling my eyes at him. "Really? Wow. You're so bad at this, Ethan! I don't even know how any girl could ever like you."

"You just said you love me," he says, smirking.

"I take it back. It was a momentary lapse in judgment."

"Can you just lay on the table?" he says. "I'm trying to give you orgasms here. You're making this way more difficult than it has to be."

"Orgasms?" I ask. That's plural; more than one. How many is more than one? Um... it could be a lot. I don't even know.

"I've finally caught your interest?" he asks. "Fuck, that was difficult. I get that you're used to being Little Miss Perfect Goodie Two Shoes, but could you calm that shit down sometimes? I need to work my magic, and it's not going to work if you keep holding back."

"I don't think you know what you're talking about," I tell him. "How are you going to give me orgasms with um... that thing? It looks like some medieval dungeon torture weapon, Ethan. You're so weird."

He plugs it into the wall, then hits a button on the handle. The entire thing starts to vibrate. This isn't some quiet, gentle, rhythmic vibration, oh, no. It's loud and shaking and I don't even know how that works because he's holding it in his hand. It kind of reminds me of a jackhammer. How loud is a jackhammer? I don't know, but I think this stupid toy of his could give it a run for its money on that count.

Stupid toy? Did I say stupid toy? Yes, well, um... Ethan is about to make me seem like the stupid one for saying that.

Ugh. Bad boys!

2 - Ethan

WHY DO GIRLS ALWAYS ARGUE when you want to give them an orgasm? That should be a nice thing, don't you think? It always starts out the same, and I thought maybe Ashley was different, but, nah, she's not.

Oh, I don't think we should! We shouldn't because of these reasons! I want to, but...

Look, Princess, just sit your sweet ass down on the pool table, lay back, spread your legs, let me see your perfect pussy, and I'll show you exactly how beautiful you are. I don't just do this for everyone, you know? Especially not now. I don't think she fully realizes it yet, and it's still hard for me to come to terms with, too, but she's the last girl I ever want to do this to again. Yeah, fuck, you can say that we're young and stupid and it's just a phase or something, but to that I can also tell you to fuck off, so I guess we're even, huh?

She thought my line was cheesy romanticism before, and it probably was, but this girl is seriously fine art at it's uh... finest. That sounded better in my head. Anyways, look, the sight of her writhing on her back, her stomach tensing, breasts heaving and swaying from her heavy breaths as she's on the brink of orgasm, it's erotic as fuck, and if anything in this world could be classified as art, I think that's exactly it. It turns me on, as if I wasn't already turned on by the sight of her naked. That's all it really takes, but this brings it to a whole new level. I didn't even know it was possible to be this excited before, but watching Ashley cum is like discovering a new planet or something. You just want to explore the fuck out of it, learn everything about it, even though you know you'll never be able to. You can try, though. You can make it your life's mission.

I'm like a fucking astronaut. This shit is serious, like NASA.

"What is that?" she asks me, making a face. "It's really loud. Is it broken?"

I laugh. Loud? Yeah, this is nothing compared to how much she'll be screaming in a couple minutes. I hope she says my name, just fucking screams it, begs me for more. There's definitely more where this came from, don't you worry, Princess. I'm already hard just thinking about burying my cock deep in her tight pussy. Fuck.

"It's not broken, Princess," I tell her. "You'll see. Just lay back and let me get to work."

You know what's better than pushing the head of your cock into a ready and waiting, soaking wet slit, though? A couple things. There's not a lot, but there's a couple things that make all the difference in the world. The first is when you're close to the person. I don't just mean you're in love with them, but when you're seriously close to them. Fuck, I've known this girl since the second grade, and we've lived in the same house for three years. Yeah, we went away to college, but it's summer now and we're back. I get that she's my stepsister and that's kind of fucked up, but whatever. Oh well. It's not like we're related. It's fine.

Yeah, so, close, intimate, that's one thing. The second is less wishy-washy and emotional. It's a thing of beauty just burying your cock inside of a girl who really really wants it, but it's even better when she's spent from already having an orgasm or two. Three? Fuck, who cares. At least one, but you hold off, don't give in, because you know it's going to be real fucking good if you just wait a second, and she cums, and you're ready, but you wait a little bit longer...

This is precision work here, for real. I can't explain the exact timing, you'll just know it when you see it. And when it happens, you move fast, deliberate, line yourself up, and push in. She's fucking soaked already, so it's easy to thrust inside of her, but she's just had an orgasm, so she's not expecting the overload of sensation, the fullness. You can see it in her eyes, see them roll into the back of her head, and you can feel it on your cock, the aftermath of her orgasm like the tremors of some personal earthquake or something. Fucking... squeezing, massaging, and she's not even sure what she wants anymore, because if you asked her before this, she'd say she was too tired to go on, but now that you're inside her, she wants more and more.

Damn fucking right, Princess. Ashley, I'm going to make you feel so fucking good...

She shivers on the pool table, fidgeting under my steady gaze and soft breath. I let out a whisper of air, breathing warmth onto her sex, and she shivers even more.

"You cold?" I ask her.

"I... a little," she says, uncertain.

"If you're too cold, we can stop," I say.

"We can't just stop!" she says.

"Oh yeah?" I ask, smirking. "You were the one trying to convince me this was a bad idea just a few seconds ago, weren't you?"

"Shut up!" she says, rolling her eyes at me.

She rolls her eyes for a different reason after I stop her with a kiss. I press the tip of my tongue against the underside of her clit, rolling it to the side, up and around her clitoral hood, then I kiss down hard on her slit, tasting her arousal.

"What were you saying?" I ask, enjoying the conflict in her eyes, the tense emotion on her face.

"You did that on purpose," she whispers, pouting at me.

"Yeah, so?"

"You're so bad, Ethan," she says. "You're the worst. Yes, this is a bad idea. It's a horrible one, alright? Are you happy now that I've admitted it? Because, what are you even going to say to our parents if they walk in on us like this?"

"I don't have to say anything to them," I say. "I'm going to say something to you instead. If you just lay back, relax, and enjoy the fuck out of this, then it'll be over faster than if you complain and whine, and then we can go upstairs, get dressed, and act more appropriately."

"You're forgetting something," she says, her voice full of sass. "You never act appropriately. That's not going to change no matter what, so I don't know why you--"

Yeah, enough of that. I smother her sex with my face, my lips, licking and tasting her. Up along her labia, first one side, then the other, teasing around her clit, but not giving her the satisfaction of a little pressure, a more direct touch. I tease and tempt her and she forgets any of what she was going to say. There you go, Princess. That's my good girl. I know I'm the bad one, but she really is so fucking good.

She's responsive, and it took me awhile to figure this out, but I think I've got it down now. She likes to move like... yeah, that's it. Her leg twitches, but I reach out and grab it, pinning it against the edge of the pool table. I drop the still-vibrating massager on the carpeted floor of the game room, letting it thud and shake down there. I've got important matters to attend to here, and I don't need that for this.

Ashley and I have some rules. Rule number one is a remnant of the past, lost and forgotten. *It's only supposed to be for a week.* Yeah, no, it's only going to be for a lot longer than that. A whole fucking lot longer. That's a null and void rule, but we've still got some that we have to adhere to.

Rule number eleven. You want to know what one? Maybe you know it already. Here it is:

"I'm going to eat your sweet fucking pussy at least once a day. At least. Maybe twice. Three times. All fucking day."

When I first made up that rule, she asked me if it was even possible. Before I met her, I would have said no. Now? Holy fuck, I can't get enough of her. She's delicious as fuck.

I stretch my tongue out and tease from the bottom of her pussy all the way up to the top, pressing inside her, tasting as much of her as I can. She flexes against me, tight, squeezing. I grab her other leg, because I'm not going to put up with her trying to stop me. It's not even her, but her body's instinctive need, her legs squeezing and clenching, trying to stop the sudden overload of sensation in her core. I need it, though. I want her to feel it. Feel me. All of it. *Just give in, Princess.*

After I pull her legs apart and lick and lap at her slit, I touch the tip of my tongue against her clit, rolling it around. She shudders beneath my touch.

"You still cold?" I ask her. "You look pretty fucking hot to me."

Her teeth chatter as she tries to think of a response. "Sh-shut up!" she yells at me.

Fuck, I love it when she gets feisty with me. I'm pretty sure my erection could rip my bathing suit to shreds, and I don't think either of us wants that. Quick, I untie them and tug on the waistband of my board shorts, pulling them down my legs. I kick them aside and grab her thighs again, then bury my face against her pussy.

She gets even more feisty. Yeah, fuck, I love it. She grabs my hair, pulling me hard, harder against her. I lick even more, harder, drinking up everything she has to offer, her arousal and her lust. I can feel her beginning to orgasm; it's close, almost there, but not quite. This is dangerous ground, but I've got to do it. I just hope she doesn't rip my hair out.

Before she realizes what's going on, I reach up and peel her fingers out of my hair, grab her wrists, then stand up fast, leaving her waiting and wanting. She bucks her hips up, trying to bring her pussy back to my face, but I'm long gone by now. This is why I needed to be careful. You know how fucking angry a woman gets when you stop right when she's on the brink of an orgasm?

Her eyes shoot open and she stares at me like a fucking banshee straight out of a horror movie. "Ethan Colton you get back down there this instant!"

"Wow!" I say, laughing at her. I know that's probably not necessary, but it's fun to see her get riled up.

"Now!" she shouts. "I was so close! Ethan..." Her voice trails off a little, softer now. What's after anger? Begging. She whimpers and pleads and gives me this cute as fuck pouty face. "Pleeaassee?"

I bend down fast and pick up the loud vibrator. She stares at it, confused, as if I didn't just show it to her a few minutes ago. "You remember this?" I ask her.

"Um... yes?" she says.

"You want to see what happens when I take this--" I heft it up, giving her a better view. "--and press it against..."

Her clit. Before I do, I turn it to the lowest setting. It's still loud, still rumbling, but I don't want to fucking destroy her with pleasure or anything. I mean, yeah, that could be fun to try sometime, but I'm pretty sure she'd accidentally kick me in the balls if I did it right now. She comes pretty fucking close to doing it anyways.

I touch the vibrating ball against her pubic mound first, letting the sensation sink into her body for a second before moving it lower. I'm careful in the beginning, because from everything I know this shit is, uh... it's a lot. How the fuck should I know how to explain it? It's just a lot, and it's beautiful to watch.

Her body shakes in time with the vibrations, trying to keep up, but she doesn't even have a chance. She grabs at the pool table, trying to dig her nails into the soft felt beneath her, but it doesn't work. She scratches and claws and when she can't squeeze or clutch anything, she gives up and latches onto her breasts, instead. I didn't expect that, but holy fuck is it hot. Her fingers dig into the soft flesh of her breasts, squeezing them, while she clenches her eyes shut.

"You like that?" I ask her.

She nods fast, super fucking fast. "M-m-mhmm..." she murmurs, her words vibrating like the toy between her legs.

I shift it a little lower, the rest of the way to her clit, and then I get ready to watch the magic. It's like fireworks, bright fucking sparks shooting into the air. Her legs kick, but I hide between them. She tries to clamp her thighs shut, but I'm standing right there so she can't. The vibrations from the toy in my hand send tremors along her legs and she shakes and kicks her feet.

Her eyes open, but she's not even looking at me. She's looking at something else entirely, and I'm pretty sure it's pure fucking bliss. Her eyes roll up and back and I see her wince. It's not pain, it's her orgasm, pleasure wrinkling her face as her body feels pure sexual release.

"Oh," she says, her lips shaped into a circle. "Oh, oh, oh my God, Ethan, I... wow... I'm cumming!"

"You want me to stop?" I ask. I'm pretty sure this is a rhetorical question. I almost laugh at the shock and horror on her face.

"No! Noo...! Holy fucking... fuck! Ethan, don't stop!"

Wow. I smile, full of pride. My good girl princess just swore. There's hope for her yet. I'll make her naughty as sin. Just in the bedroom, though. Or, you know, behind closed doors because we aren't in a bedroom right now. I like how she's prim and proper and good when we're in public. I love that she's a good girl to everyone else, but she's a naughty fucking dirty girl just for me.

"Ethan!" she screeches, but it's quiet, lost, panting. "I... tooooo much, please...?"

I ease up, but just a little. Fuck, that was on the lowest setting. What more do you want from me? I pull the round head of the vibrator away from her beautiful fucking pussy and let her relax for a second.

"Ohmygod," she says, fast, all in one word. "Ethan, ohmygod what was that?"

"An orgasm," I tell her, in case she forgot.

She laughs. She laughs more than she should, like I've just told the funniest joke in the world. It's beautiful, too. Her orgasm was fine art, but seeing her naked and laughing in front of me is complete-ly unexplainable. It's beauty and purity in its finest form, and it's mine, it's because of me, and she's giving that to me, she gave herself to me.

"Can..." She gives me a shy, tentative look, gazing at me through sultry, yet demure eyelashes. "Can you do it again?"

"You better lay the fuck down," I tell her, smirking. "That was the lowest setting, and I'm turning it up."

"No way! What? The lowest?"

"Mhm," I murmur. "You ready?"

"I... I don't think... no! Ethan, don't turn it up! I'm going to break! You're going to break me!"

"Oh, I'll fucking break you alright," I tell her.

She laughs and squirms and tries to get away from me, but I grab her leg and keep her in place. I turn the setting on the vibrator up a little. Just a little, alright? Fuck, I don't want to break her! Our parents are coming home today, so it's not like I can leave her in a puddle of naked ecstasy. Yeah, it sounds like a good time, but how the fuck would I explain that to her mom?

"Eth--" She starts to say my name, but she stops. You want to know why? Because I touch the heavy vibrations of the round head of the toy against her stomach, then smooth it down towards her clit.

She's done. This girl is completely fucking done. And she's mine.

I smile at her and whisper the words, "I love you, Ashley," but I know she can't hear me. She's too lost in ecstasy. I'll tell her again later, though, don't worry.

3 - Ashley

I AM DESTROYED. I don't think I exist anymore. I'm pretty sure I've melted. I didn't even know something like this was possible, but Ethan's shown me that a lot of things I never thought possible are definitely possible, so...

I guess the first was when he stopped being a jerk and showed me his soft side. Yes, he's still kind of a bad boy, but he's my bad boy and he's gentle and nice, though still a bit rough and rude, too. I don't think he's being gentle or nice right now, though. Oh, no, this is completely rough and rude and I do not even know how any of this works, but it's amazing.

My body shivers and trembles. I thought it would take longer. I don't know why I thought that, but after one orgasm, I thought it would take a little longer to reach another, except as soon as he touched the vibrating head of his toy to my clit, I was done. I'm still done. My body shakes, muscles I didn't even know I had start to tense and flex, and I think I just had another orgasm, except I'm not sure, because it might have been two back to back. One or two or... three?

How is that even possible? I don't even know, but this toy of his is kind of amazing. My body aches. It's... I need a break, I need to stop. As soon as I think I can't take anymore, as soon as I'm about to beg him to stop, he does.

Oh, he's very good at this. He knows me, doesn't he? I don't know how, because I feel like I don't even know myself, but Ethan knows exactly what to do and exactly when to do it. That's what it seems like, though I know he's not always like that. There's a few things that we're figuring out how to do together, one of which is what happens after sex.

Sex? Um... did we.. is what we just did considered sex? I want to cuddle with him and hold him and no sooner than I think this, he's in my arms. Dreamy and sweet, I wrap my arms around him and kiss and cuddle him.

Not so dreamy and sweet, he nudges my legs open, plants himself firmly between them, and guides his rock hard cock inside me. One moment I'm kissing him, and the next I'm letting out a sharp gasp at the fullness of him inside me.

"Oh... oh, Ethan, I'm..."

"Yeah," he says. "I get it. I know. You're sore, huh? I'll be gentle with you, Princess. I just need to feel your sweet fucking pussy around me. Please?"

He pushes more inside of me, careful, until he's all the way in, then he rocks back and forth a little, delicate. I guess it's delicate, except for the fact that he's incredibly hard. I... I like it, though. I didn't get to feel this when he had the vibrator pressed tight against my clit, forcing rough pleasure through my body. This is soft and gentle, though hard and deliberate, too. It's... kind of like cuddling? Sex-cuddling? Is that a thing?

"Alright," I say, kissing him. I want to kiss him more, on the lips, and he kisses me back, too.

"Fuck, you feel so good," he says, pulling out of me almost all the way. When he pushes back in, he's a little rougher than before. The sound of his skin slapping against mine echoes through the game room. I can feel the pool table shake beneath us, the legs creaking.

"Gentle," I say, grinning. I want to see what he'll do.

"I'm trying!" he says, grinning back at me. "Fuck, I just..."

His lips crash onto mine, kissing me. This is his distraction, I think. It's his way of trying to keep me preoccupied so he can... *oh yes...*

He pulls out and thrusts hard into me. I don't mean to, but my body gives in to him, too. I was cumming hard just a few seconds ago, and it's what my body remembers, it's what it wants to keep doing. I squeeze and clutch against his cock inside me, tremors of my previous orgasm massaging Ethan's shaft. He trembles a little, and I feel him twitch inside me, filling me even more.

I can't stop now. Each time his cock twitches, I squeeze back in return. I don't mean to, it just... it happens. It's weird, like an out of body experience, but I can feel every smooth sensation of it, too. Instinct and need kick in, and apparently my body knows exactly what to do. It's a sore, dull, aching pleasure, but it's wonderful and amazing, too.

"How do I feel?" I ask him, whispering into his ear, then nipping his earlobe. "Tell me what it feels like when you're inside me. I want to know."

"Fuck, Princess, do we really have to do this right now?"

I nip harder at his ear, biting it. Ethan grunts, slamming hard into me. "Yes," I say, whispering. "Tell me. Please, Ethan?"

"It's..." He's at a loss for words for a second while he pulls out and thrusts back in. "Fuck, it's tight," he says finally. "It's fucking smooth, too. I can feel each time you squeeze, and it's sexy as fuck. I love watching you cum, Princess. You're so fucking beautiful. I want to cum inside you."

I try to think of something. I'm not very good at this, though. Ethan's a lot better. What is dirty talk? What do you say? Um...

I just say the first thing I can think of that sounds kind of exciting to me.

"I'm not on the pill anymore, though," I tell him. "Ethan you can't cum inside me. I'll get pregnant."

He blinks, confused, but his cock throbs inside me, excited. Does he like that?

I grab his hips and pull him further in me.

"Are you serious?" he asks.

"Oh! Oh, Ethan! Don't cum inside me! What are you doing?"

Yes, um... so this is kind of exaggerated and played up, but I hope he gets the point. I think he does, because right after I say that he slams into me as hard as he can.

Growling into my ear, he says, "Oh yeah? You're mine, Princess, and I'll do whatever the fuck I want."

"You can't!" I say. And um... well, that's the last of that, because he just um...

Ethan is very persuasive, and he distracts me, and I forget everything but the feeling of him inside of me, because it feels so right and good.

I hear something else. I feel like this is important somehow, and I can hear something. Um... someone? Calling our names. I think. Who is that? Is that...

I'm about to cum, though. Again. Holy wow! I'm glad I didn't say that out loud, because I"m pretty sure Ethan would have made fun of me. *Did you just say holy wow? Shut up, Ethan!* Yes, best not to do that.

And... he's done. He pushes hard into me, filling me with his cock, then filling me with his seed. I feel it, feel his warmth and the heat of his release and his cock, and I follow soon after. My body squeezes against him and I press my fingers into his hips, my fingernails raking against his tight, muscular butt. Oh, I love it. Ethan plays football, and he's got the muscles and body to prove it, and currently those muscles and that body are pressed hard against me and on top of me, and...

I really can't get rid of this strange feeling that there's something... wrong? My body doesn't want to believe it, though, just wants to milk this pleasure for all its worth, and it does, but then I panic.

I panic because it's my mom, and Ethan's dad, and they're calling our names.

"Ashley?" my mom says.

"Ethan!" my stepdad shouts out. "Where are you two? Anybody home?"

"Oh, shit," Ethan says, expression blank.

"Oh my god oh my god get off of me!" I shout at him, slapping his arms, pushing him away.

He moves, fast, landing quick on his feet. Oh no, what are we supposed to do? They're close, too! I can hear them getting closer, hear them walking down the hall towards the game room. This is like some horrifying version of Marco Polo that you play in the pool, except if they catch us naked I'm pretty sure it's going to end up being a lot worse than a simple "tag, you're it!"

Ethan pulls on his swim trunks fast and then flings my bikini top and bottoms at me. I panic and pull the bottoms on quick, but they're backwards. Oh my God, seriously? I slip them down my legs again, and put them on the right way this time, all while I can hear our parents just outside in the hall. Thankfully the door is closed, so I guess we have a little more time.

The vibrator is on the floor.

"Ethan!" I hiss at him. "The... that thing!"

"What thing?" he asks. "Damnit, put your top on!"

"Shut up, I'm doing it!" I tell him, trying to be quiet. It's not working at all, but at least I'm putting my top on. I scramble with the back of it, tying it in place. Um... it's a bit loose, but I guess it's good enough.

They open the door. Ethan stands there, nothing doing. I don't even know how he does it. I spin around and face our parents with um... dignity?

This is a little embarrassing, but I think it might be fine. They both know, right? Ethan called my mom and asked her if he could date me a few days ago, and she said she'd talk to his dad, so it should be fine and they both know. If that's true, why is my mom staring at us with a look of abject horror, then?

Um... I don't think this is fine.

Ethan's dad glances between the two of us, one eyebrow raised. "What are you two doing in here?" he asks.

I give my mom a look. THE LOOK! Yes, that look. She mouths an apology, lips moving as if to say "I didn't have time to tell him."

Then she gives *me* a look! It's a look that questions why we're doing sexy things in the pool room, to which I really don't have an answer, because I most definitely told Ethan we shouldn't do this.

And also the vibrator is on the floor by his feet, not even hidden. It's off now, and thankfully his dad doesn't see it, but when I look down to glance at it, my mom's eyes follow mine, and she claps her hand over her mouth after she realizes it. If there was any plausible deniability before this, there's definitely none left.

Yes, Mom, Ethan and I were just having dirty sex with sex toys and multiple orgasms while on the pool table. Also, and this is super terrible, but I can see a wet spot on the pool table just near the edge which is completely sex juices things, and if that wasn't bad enough, I can feel Ethan's cum inside me, which is sometimes kind of sexy, but I don't even know how to explain that if it starts leaking out and down my leg.

Basically this is all horrible and mortifying and I can't even believe she didn't tell Ethan's dad yet! That just makes it worse!

Ugh.

UGH!

4 - Ethan

ASHLEY KEEPS GIVING ME THIS LOOK. What's up with that? I don't even know what kind of look this is, either. It's not a sexy look, that's for sure. Sometimes when she's really excited for something, you can see her eyes widen a little, and her eyebrows lift up slightly, almost like she's surprised or shocked, and then there's this cute little twitch of her lips, just in the corner. That's about how far she gets before I jump on her and kiss the fuck out of her.

Or do other things. You know, the kinds of things that get me in trouble. Like now.

Oh! Fuck. So it's that kind of look, huh? Yeah, fuck you too, Princess. This isn't just on me. It takes two to tango, so don't you be giving me that look. It takes two to fuck the shit out of each other, too. I think I prefer sex to dancing, but what do I know?

Shit, she's still giving me that look. I don't even know why anymore. Yeah yeah, I get it, we're in trouble, and...

"What were you two doing?" my dad asks.

I open my mouth to say something, but then I stop. Ashley's mom is giving me a look now. What's up with these looks? It's like they don't want me to say...

Holy fuck! That's it! My dad doesn't know. So uh... yeah... I don't want to be the one to tell him this. I mean, if I have to, I guess I'll do it. Take one for the team, right? I'd just rather not do it right now when Ashley and I were having sex on the pool table a few seconds ago. I glance over to it quickly and see the telltale signs of my sexy little Princess's wet arousal on the edge of the pool table. It's kind of hot, or it would be really hot if my dad wasn't standing right there. He puts his hand on the edge of the pool table, his fingers mere inches away from the wetness.

Well, fuck.

"Vacuuming," I say quick. Yeah, that's it. Cleaning. We were cleaning. Makes sense. Complete and perfect sense.

"You were vacuuming?" my dad asks, giving me a strange look.

Shit, this doesn't make any sense. When was the last time I vacuumed? When was the last time I did any cleaning whatsoever. Fuck. We hire someone to come once a week to clean the place up, so why would I even be vacuuming?

"Ethan was screwing around watching TV and he had a bowl of chips and he dropped it," Ashley says, covering for me.

Wait a second. Covering for me? She just ratted me out. What a... well, I was going to say bitch, but nah, she's not. I glance over at her and give her a dirty look, because I think that's how we're supposed to be playing this off, acting like we hate each other again, but then I can't stop looking at her. That is one sexy as fuck bikini she has on. It's even sexier considering it's hanging loose around her chest since she didn't have time to tie it tight. Man, this girl has some curves to her. Nothing crazy, but they're soft and sensual and when I look at her I just want to grab her and squeeze the fuck out of her and then...

Fuck. Cut it out, Ethan. I mentally slap myself. Ashley, stepsister, dad, stepmother, stop ogling, pull it together.

This is like football, right? Yeah, that's it. What play are we running? Um... well, I kind of want to go for a touchdown. Run my cock straight past Ashley's defensive line and into her end zone. By that I mean bend her over and take her from behind. Not anal sex. Unless she wants to try it. I'm open to the possibility.

My dad is staring at me again. Shit.

"Ethan, are you alright?" he asks.

"He's been such a jerk the entire time you've been gone," Ashley says.

My stepmom chimes in now, too. "That must have been what those noises were, honey," she says to my dad. "Remember, you were wondering what was going on in here?"

My dad shrugs and grunts, gruff. "It did sound strange. I thought Ethan had a girl over at first, but I'm glad that's not the case."

I die. I am pretty fucking sure I'm dead right now. A girl over? Nah, I was just fucking Ashley. Don't even worry about it, dad.

Ashley dies, too. Her face is pale and she looks like she's going to pass out. I need to fix this. I shift to the side and bump my hip against hers, pushing her against the edge of the pool table. She squeaks and glares at me and shouts out in protest. Yeah, that's it, say my name, Princess. Fuck, I love it.

I'd love it more if it were under different circumstances, but whatever.

"Ethan!" she shouts at me.

"Look, Little Miss Perfect," I tell her. "I told you not to get in my way. I was trying to clean. I get it, alright? Yeah, I shouldn't have brought those chips in here. Should have stayed cleaner. Maybe gotten some carrot sticks or something. Whatever. You don't have to get on my case about it."

She gives me a dirty look that's also halfway between a sad pout. Well, yeah, sorry? I don't want to yell at her or anything, but it's kind of necessary right now.

I hope my dad's buying it. He doesn't look like he's buying it.

"Where's the vacuum?" he says. He glances down at the same time and scuffs his foot against the carpet. "You did a terrible job, Ethan. If you're going to bother cleaning, the least you could do is actually clean."

"Yeah, Ethan!" Ashley says, making a face at me and sticking out her tongue.

Oh, you don't even want to do that, Princess. I *will* make you regret it. Or, I would, but uh... yeah, my dad's here.

"Fine, fine," I say. "Whatever, I'll do it again." I go to get the vacuum cleaner, but then I realize I don't even know where it is. I glance to Ashley for help, and she gives me a weird look.

What's with all these looks! Seriously, these people are crazy. I'm not the crazy one here.

"I put the vacuum cleaner away in the--" I say, prompting her.

She stares at me blankly, completely not even prompted at all.

"--in the..." I say again, slowly.

"Oh!" The lights turn on, Ashley is here with me again. "You put it in the closet, idiot."

Wow. Fucking wow. Idiot? Wow.

I go to the closet, open it, and find the vacuum cleaner standing right there. It's some huge monstrosity of a machine. I didn't even know vacuum cleaners could get this big. I lug it out, go to plug it in again, but I trip on something on the way there.

It turns on. Vrrrrooooo.

It's not the vacuum cleaner, though.

The vibrator I was using on Ashley just minutes before flares to life after I tripped over it and starts bumbling and shaking around on the carpet. Shit, that's loud, isn't it? I guess I was too preoccupied before with wanting to see Ashley space out in ecstatic glee, but now that things have sort of settled, it's definitely loud. I scramble quick before anyone notices and plug the vacuum cleaner in, then slam my foot down on the power pedal to turn it on.

Vrrrooooooo.

You know what I want to know? Simple question, not so simple answer: Why is the vibrator louder than the vacuum cleaner? The sound of it thumping and shaking on the carpet is definitely overpowering the rhythmic thrum of the vacuum cleaner's motor, and I have have no idea how this works. Ashley stumbles to the ground and grabs the vibrator fast, keeping it hidden under the pool table, then she pulls on the cord, ripping the plug from the wall.

My dad stares at the two of us like we're on drugs, but I don't think he's noticed our sexual predicament yet.

"I don't know what's going on, but I'm tired and I'm going to go take a nap," he says. "I hope you two settle down and figure everything out by the time I get up. I don't want to have to deal with constant arguments after just getting home. I had to deal with enough of that in endless business meetings the past few days. Are we all on the same page here?"

"Yeah," I say. "Got it, Dad."

"Yes," Ashley says. "Ethan and I will try to get along."

You know how we could get along, Princess? If we just go upstairs and fuck for days in my room.

I'm supposed to be vacuuming, aren't I? I move the vacuum back and forth a little. How do you even vacuum? I have no idea. I feel kind of dumb, because this seems like it should be easy, but uh... fuck if I know.

Ashley gives me a dirty look and swipes the vacuum cleaner away from me, then gets to work. I watch her, admiring her from afar. I wish I could say I was admiring her handiwork, but, nah, I'm staring at her ass.

I can do that now. It's fine. My dad's gone. He left to go take a nap, remember?

Except uh...

"Ethan, can you please stop staring at my daughter's butt when I'm in the room?"

Shit.

"Sorry," I say. "She's just got a really nice ass."

Ashley turns around and slaps my shoulder. "Ethan! Seriously? I can't believe you said that in front of my mom!"

"Look," I tell her. "I was taught that if you can't say anything nice, you shouldn't say anything at all."

"I have no idea what you're saying right now," Ashley says, glaring at me.

"If your ass wasn't nice, I would have kept my mouth shut," I say, doing the deductive reasoning for her. "Thankfully it's sexy as fuck, so I was more than happy to compliment you."

They both groan. Mother and daughter. I didn't even know synchronized groaning was a real thing. "Ethan..."

Ashley's mom comes over to me and holds out her arms. Uh... hug? I hug her, and she hugs me back.

"I appreciate your appreciation of my daughter," she says. "Please don't forget that I'm your stepmother now, though. Can we keep things a little under wraps when we're all together?"

"Are you talking about using condoms?" I ask.

Apparently this is not even close to what we're talking about.

"Oh my God," my stepmom says. "You... you two... haven't... Ashley, are you pregnant?" she asks, turning to her daughter. "Please, tell me you aren't. I mean, if... no. I was going to say if it's with Ethan it's alright, but, no, I'm sorry, it's not. Ethan, please understand that I love you, but I'm going to kill you now."

"Whoa, hold up!" I say. "She's on the pill!" I think. Fuck. I turn to Ashley. "You're on the pill, right? I don't want to die, Princess. Please tell me you're on the pill. You were joking before, right?"

Ashley blushes, cheeks red as fuck. Shit, she's beautiful. She's so cute and innocent sometimes, but this girl is definitely not cute and innocent when it counts. I've seen what she can do. I saw her deepthroat my cock one time. I saw her writhing and thrashing on the pool table earlier while I sent roaring ecstasy surging through her body. I've seen her have quite a few orgasms this past week, and I'm pretty sure good girls like Ashley Banks don't tend to get that wild and crazy in bed.

Or not in bed. Really, half the times we've had sex haven't even been in bed. Half? That's a rough estimate. To be honest, I haven't been keeping track.

"Be... fore?" her mom asks. "It's true, isn't it? You two were having sex in here, weren't you?"

I shrug, nonchalant, nothing doing.

Ashley just kind of whimpers. "Mom, I told him it was a bad idea."

"We really need to set some ground rules here," her mom says. "First off, no having sex in the common areas. Your father and I don't have sex on the pool table, Ethan, and I expect you'll adhere to the same sense of decency."

"Alright," I say. "Sorry." It's a fair request, you know? Not much I can do to fight that one.

"As for... for the other thing," Ashley's mom says. "Are you two serious about each other? I need to know if this is going to be a loving and lasting relationship."

"Mom, I'm not pregnant," Ashley says.

"Good," my stepmom says. "I didn't want to have to castrate Ethan. I've grown fond of him these past few years."

I laugh, because she's joking, right? She doesn't laugh. Ashley doesn't laugh, either. They both stare at me with these haunted, hollow eyes, almost as if they both belong in a horror movie and I'm about to be the first one to die. Fuck.

Ashley's mom grins at me, and it's creepy as fuck. "Now," she says, "if you're both committed to one another--"

"I'm committed," I say, fast. I don't want to die. I won't go down like in a horror movie. This is not how my life plays out.

Also I really like Ashley. Fuck, I love her. I'm not just saying that because her mom said she was going to castrate me, either.

"I think he's telling the truth," Ashley says to her mom, nodding. "I believe him."

"How can you tell, though?" her mom asks. "I don't know if you realize this, but Ethan's kind of a bad boy."

"You both realize I'm standing right here, don't you?" I ask.

"Shush, dear," my stepmom says. "Not now."

"He really is nice to me, mom," Ashley says. "The other night we went out to a fancy restaurant. Ethan got dressed up and everything, too. Just a tie, not a full suit, but I liked it. Have you ever seen him do that for someone else?"

"It could be a ruse," her mother says. "What else? Tell me more."

"We've made breakfast together every day, and he makes me pancakes."

"Ooh... pancakes, really? That's something, isn't it?"

"They're different every day, too! It is, it's really nice. And we cuddle and watch TV, or we go swimming. It's not even, um... alright, can I tell you something?"

I'm not even here, apparently. I lean against the pool table and wait to be invited back to the conversation.

"Yes, of course, you can tell me anything," her mom says.

"Um... well... the sex is um... it's good. Very very good. Except it's different, too. Ethan is really um... nice? Considerate, er... but rough, and um... I don't want to go into details there, but..."

"Look," I say, because I can't keep quiet any-more. "I don't know what kind of fucked up guys have ignored the fact that you're beautiful, perfect, sexy, intelligent, amazing, cute, funny, adorable, gorgeous, your body is fine as hell, and seriously you're just perfect, but uh... they're all stupid as fuck, and I feel like I'm the last person in the world who should be the one to tell you this, but yeah, you're perfect. I know a good thing when I see it, Princess, and I'd never treat you like anything less than a Queen. I'm not stupid. Any guy would be lucky to be with you. If you want to be with me, I'm not going to take that for granted."

Apparently I've just said something good, because they're both beaming at me now, smiles from ear to ear.

Her mom nods twice, then says, "Good. I approve. As long as you're both careful and have a legitimate form of birth control, I won't pry about the specifics."

"You know I'm careful, Mom," Ashley says. "I take my pills every day. I promise. It's just... I know Ethan has, um... a past..."

"If you give my daughter an STD or break her heart, I'm going to castrate you," Ashley's mom says, and she says it with this grin that makes it seem like she's happy, but that's the least happy thing I can think of someone ever saying.

"I get tested," I tell her. "Uh... it's my dad's thing, he makes me, because of the same reasons. I swear I wouldn't screw around with something like that. I've always used condoms with every girl except Ashley, and I haven't had sex with anyone but her since the last time I was tested, so..."

"I think that's enough of that for now," her mom says. "Let's go make a snack. Are you two hungry? I haven't had anything to eat since a few hours before we got on the plane and I'm famished. Oh, we should talk about the camping trip, too. Your father still wants us all to go, Ethan. I hope you haven't forgotten?"

"Camping trip?" Ashley asks. "Oh, are we really doing that?"

"Camping is serious," I tell her. "We don't joke around with camping here."

"It is," my stepmom says. "Which is why I thought that we could all have a family sit down once we got there and break the news to your father."

"What news?" I ask.

They both sigh and shake their heads. What? I don't think I like this. They're way too close. I'm not that close with my dad. You know what would happen if I tried to talk to my dad about sex?

Something bad. Or weird. Or terrible. I have no idea. I don't even want to try to find out.

Mia Clark

5 - Ashley

I TOLD MY MOM I WAS just going to go up and change into regular clothes really quick, since I'm still wearing my bathing suit, but maybe this was a bad idea.

Do you want to know why it's a bad idea? It's not hard to guess.

Ethan. Ethan Colton. My stepbrother, and my boyfriend. Yes, anything involving him always turns into a bad idea. I don't even know how I got involved with him in the first place. He's an absolute menace!

I really do like him, but I'm trying to change here, and I didn't expect an audience.

"What are you even doing?" I ask him.

He's sitting at the foot of my bed, watching me go through my closet to pick out clothes. "Just hanging out," he says.

"Ethan, I'm trying to change. I'm about to go right back downstairs. Didn't you tell my mom you were coming up to change, too?"

"Yeah, that's what I told her," he says, shrugging. "Just calm yourself down there, Princess. I'll go change in a second."

"In a second after... what?" I ask. "Because we're not going to have sex up here. You do realize that, right?"

He gives me that patented bad boy grin of his. "Nah, I bet I could make you change your mind."

"You probably could!" I say, exasperated. Then I laugh. "Ethan, we really can't, though. We... I don't know when we can again, but we can't right now. It's kind of weird, don't you think?"

"What, because of our parents being right downstairs?" he asks. "We did it before, Princess. What's the big deal?"

"Um... because my mom knows?"

"So it was cool when she didn't know, but now that she does know, we're never going to have sex again?"

"Ugh! Is that all I am to you, Ethan Colton? Some girl to have sex with?"

He grins again, clearly amused. "Nah. It's not just sex." Then, with a completely straight face, he adds, "I want to fuck that gorgeous perfect pussy of yours, too. That's different from sex. Real raw and primal, on a totally different level."

"Why am I even dating you?" I ask, rolling my eyes at him. "You're not very romantic. You're going to have to work on wooing me better if you want this to last. Also, what about making love? We can do that too now, you know? It doesn't always have to be--"

This was apparently a bad thing to say, because no sooner than I say it, while my back is turned and I'm picking out a cute shirt from my closet, Ethan comes up behind me. He puts his hands on my hips, pulling me towards him while stepping even closer to me, and he softly kisses my neck. I melt under his touch and his lips, my knees buckling.

Wow. That's... *wow.*

He's really soft and sweet when he wants to be, which is the entire problem with all of this. He's just... everything. I don't even know how, but he's confident and cocky, but also sweet and nice. He's gentle and careful and considerate, but he also knows how to push my limits in a way that I enjoy. It's not too much, it's just enough, and if you told me before that I would love being handled roughly, and then treated softly, sometimes back to back, I would have probably told you that you're crazy, but...

No, it's true. I love it. I didn't ever think I'd fall in love with someone like Ethan, but I have.

"Do you love me?" I ask him, leaning my head back and nuzzling against his shoulder.

He moves his hands from my hips to my bare stomach, criss-crossing his fingers over my belly button. His lips trail soft kisses up my neck, to my ear, sweet and gentle.

"Yeah, I do," he says. He's not cocky or playful or acting like a jerk anymore. He's serious and sincere, and that, too, catches me off guard. "Listen, Princess," he says. "I don't know what it is, but I can't get enough of you. I just want to touch you and keep you close, and yeah, I want to be inside you, too, but it's not just that. I want to talk to you. I want to get to know you better. I know a lot, but I want to know more, alright? I want to cuddle and watch movies and all of that boyfriend and girlfriend shit people do."

I laugh and nuzzle against him more, then turn to look over my shoulder, tipping my chin up. He kisses me quick on the lips.

"*Boyfriend and girlfriend shit?*" I ask. "You were really doing well there for a second."

"Fuck," he says, grinning. "I have no idea how to do any of this, Ashley. You're going to have to teach me. You're the smart one, right?"

"You can't play that game with me, Ethan Colton," I tell him, wrinkling my nose. "I know you're not stupid, no matter what you want everyone else to think."

"Nah," he says.

"Nah!" I say back to him, sticking out my tongue. "You're on your own, lover boy. I'm not going to teach you how to do anything."

"Wow," he says, smirking. "I can't believe this. I thought we were close. Aren't you supposed to be my stepsister or something?"

"Gross," I say. "You're so weird. Do you like that? Does it turn you on to think about sticking your hard cock into your stepsister's tight little pussy?"

"Holy fuck where did that come from? Is this a porn movie or something?"

"Might as well be!" I say, laughing. "Oh my God where did you find that vibrator thing?"

"Oh, you liked that?" he asks. "Yeah, that's for special use. We won't be using that any time soon. Sad as fuck, that's what that is."

"It's kind of loud. It was louder than the vacuum cleaner. It felt so... so good, though. I can't even explain it."

"You're going to dump me for a vibrator, aren't you?" he asks. "I'll never be good enough for you again."

"No," I say. "I'll keep you around. I can't cuddle with a vibrator, now can I?"

"That's cold, Princess. Is that all I'm good for now? Cuddling?"

"I'm sure I can think of some other uses for you..." I say. Quick, I reach behind me and put my hand on the crotch of his bathing suit. He twitches in response. He wasn't erect before, but I bet I could get him that way in a matter of seconds.

It's sexy and empowering in a way. This is for me and me alone, and I have complete control over

Ethan's arousal. Sort of. I mean, once he's aroused, he um... takes complete control of me, so I don't know how that works or who is in control of what, but it's still fun and exciting either way.

He surprises me by pulling my hand away. "Hey, calm yourself," he says.

"You're telling me to calm myself?" I ask, laughing. "I think you're the one getting excited over here."

"Yeah," he says, kissing my neck. "And I'd like nothing more than to pick you up, toss you onto the bed, and bury my cock inside you, baby girl, but your mom's waiting for us and I don't want to be rude."

"I think that's what bad boys do, though," I say, playing Devil's Advocate. "It's in your job description: Be as rude as you can, as often as possible."

"Maybe," he says. "How about good girls? What are they supposed to do?"

"Become corrupted by bad boys," I say. "Haven't you even read the bad boy handbook, Ethan? Gosh!"

He laughs loudly and spins me around, keeping his hands tight on me. He kisses me softly, then a little more, a little little more, and his fingers creep down my butt until he has a handful, which he squeezes. I put my arms around him and hold him tight and kiss him back. I squeeze his butt, too. I'm allowed to, because I'm his girlfriend, right? If he can squeeze mine, I can squeeze his, and since we're dating I can still be a good girl at the same time. I'm pretty sure that's how this works.

"I like that shirt you picked out," he tells me. "You should wear these shorts, too." He lets go of my hip with one hand and reaches past me into my closet, grabbing a pair of shorts hanging up. "They'd look cute together."

"Cute?" I ask. "What if I want to be sexy?"

"You're always sexy, Princess, but there's nothing sexy about the clothes in your closet. Not that I'm complaining. Makes it fun to take your clothes off. It's like unwrapping a present."

"Well," I tell him, rolling my eyes. "I don't think I want to show you the lingerie I bought last week, then. If you don't think I have any sexy clothes, I just don't want to show you them. You don't deserve it."

His ears perk up and his eyes widen. "You bought sexy lingerie?" he asks.

I nod, fast. "Mhm, but not for you."

"Who's it for if it's not for me?" he asks. "I need to know who I'm about to beat up."

"It's just for me. Me and... um... Wallace."

"Who the fuck is Wallace?" Ethan asks, one eyebrow raised.

"I don't know. It's the first name I could think of. It's that vibrator toy thing you used on me. What is that? I've never seen a vibrator that big before."

"What kind of vibrators have you even seen?" Ethan asks, eyebrow still raised. "I thought you were the good girl here. I might have to change my opinion of you."

"I have one," I say, whispering to him. "It's hidden, though."

"Oh yeah?" he asks.

"It's not as strong as the one you showed me. It's a lot smaller, but... it's quieter, too, um... I like it..."

"It's here?"

"Yup."

"Can you show me?" he asks. "Later, not now. I want you to show me how you use it."

"Will you use it on me, too?" I ask him. "Um... does that sound weird? I know we could just have sex, but I think it sounds fun if we, er... no, that's weird, huh?"

"Nah," he says, smiling at me. "Ashley, we're still going to play by the rules, just in a different way. Boyfriend with benefits rules now, not the stepbrother with benefits ones. They're mostly all the same, though. This is supposed to be fun, right?"

I nod, smiling back at him. "That's rule number six."

"If you want to have fun like that, with some toys, we can have fun like that."

"What if I want to have fun by putting my clothes on and going downstairs to make food with my mom because she's going to wonder why we've been up here for so long?" I ask.

"Wow, that's harsh. I'm trying to be a good boyfriend here and you're just knocking me down each step of the way."

"Because you're being bad, Ethan!" I say, laughing at him. "You need to go get dressed, too, alright? Then go downstairs. I... um... I'm going to take a shower, quick, too."

"What, why?" he asks. "You can't tell me to go away and then tell me you're going to take a shower. That's like torture. I'm going to die."

"Oh, poor baby. Does your penis hurt from being too erect?"

He bites his bottom lip, pretending to whimper, and nods.

"You're so dumb. I'm taking a shower because, um... there's your stuff in me, and er..."

Without warning, Ethan slips his hand down the front of my bikini bottoms and cups my pussy, sneaking a finger inside me. Which isn't even that difficult to do, because of his own personal lubricant. Which is exactly the reason I wanted to take a shower, except now he's fingering me. Why is he doing this? Ugh!

Why do I like it? Well, I know why I like it, so that's a stupid question to ask myself, don't you think?

"Yeah, definitely could use some cleaning," Ethan says, matter-of-fact. "You're leaking."

"I was just about to give in and let you have your way with me, but not after you say something like that," I tell him, trying to sound indignant. The truth of the matter is I kind of don't want him to stop, though. I like his finger inside me, with the heel of his palm pressed against my clit...

He pulls it out, though. "That was all a part of my plan," he says. "One of us had to put a temporary stop to this irresistible attraction going on between us."

"Oh, is that it?" I ask.

"Yeah, that's it, Princess," Ethan says, grinning. "Alright, I'm going to go get dressed now. You hurry up with that shower and meet me downstairs. I'll be waiting for you."

"And I'll be waiting for tonight so that I can show you how I use my secret toys," I tell him, winking and blowing him a kiss as he walks away, heading to my door.

"Wow," Ethan says, sighing and shaking his head. He gives me one last look before opening my bedroom door and stepping outside. "Wow, wow, wow," he continues, walking down the upstairs hall towards his bedroom. "I can't believe this. I've created a monster."

Yes, well, maybe he has. What of it?

I can be a monster if I want to, and if I'm going to be one, it's going to be while I'm wearing sexy lingerie with my little private toys, with Ethan waiting and watching me from a short distance.

I hurry over and close my door, then lock it for good measure. Better safe than sorry. I really do have to hurry, and um...

I'm excited about Ethan, and our relationship, and how everything's been going this past week, even if we've only really been dating for the past few days, but I'm excited to see my mom again, too. It's kind of weird, but I'm excited to see Ethan's dad, too.

I just hope he understands, though. I don't know what we're going to do if he doesn't.

Mia Clark

6 - Ethan

ASHLEY'S STILL GETTING DRESSED or showering or something, but I figure I should go downstairs instead of putting myself in a position of wanting to take my pants off. I mean, fuck, I just put these pants on, so I should probably keep them on for, uh... I don't know, what's a good amount of time? Depends on the situation, really.

If I'm downstairs with Ashley's mom, making a snack, then I'm good for awhile.

If I hang around upstairs and just so happen to find myself in Ashley's room when she steps out of the shower, giving me a show of her slippery wet, naked body, uh... yeah, two seconds or less is about how long my pants will stay on then.

I choose to go downstairs. Yeah, let's go with that. I choose to go downstairs because she locked me out of her room. I can't even believe this girl. I thought we had something together. Boyfriend and girlfriend? Seriously, what's up with that? I don't know exactly how this is supposed to work, but I'm pretty sure the girlfriend girl in this relationship isn't supposed to lock the boyfriend guy out of her room. I'm pretty sure that's the opposite of what's supposed to happen, actually.

I'm going to have to have a serious talk with her about this later. Ashley, please keep your bedroom door unlocked so I can come in whenever I want and ravage the fuck out of your shower-soaked body. Thanks for understanding, Princess.

Oh well. It's cool. Her mom's fun and nice, too, and I really should ease up a bit on Ashley. What's that saying? Anticipation makes the wait more exciting or something. If you ask me, I think that's a bunch of bullshit, because seriously what's more exciting than thrusting my raging hard-on into Ashley's arousal-slick pussy? If there's something more exciting than that, I have no idea. If you try to tell me there's something more exciting than that, I'm probably going to have to call you a liar.

Yeah, whatever. Anyways, I go downstairs to the kitchen, instead. Ashley's mom is standing by the counter with a few bowls and some vegetables nearby. She's chopping a cucumber, but she stops and smiles at me as I walk in.

"Hey," I say. "What's up?"

"Hello, yourself," my stepmom says. "You sure took a long time up there..."

"Yeah, uh... I was helping Ashley pick out some clothes?" I say. That sounds good, right? Fuck if I know.

"Is that what you kids are calling it nowadays?" she asks.

Oh, well, if we're being honest, uh...

"Seriously, she cockblocked me," I tell her. "Your daughter's a tease."

"Ethan!" my stepmom says. She looks like she's caught between wanting to laugh at me and being a little upset. Yeah yeah, I get it. What do you want me to do about it?

"Sorry," I say. "I don't know how this is supposed to work."

She shrugs. "Do you want to talk about it?"

"Uh... about what?"

She shrugs again. "I know Ashley's my daughter, but you're my stepson now, so you can talk to me about things like that if you want. If you'd like to, that is. If you need a mother's opinion? I don't want to pressure you or seem like I'm trying to push into your life and be a mother figure if you'd rather I didn't, though. It's up to you, Ethan."

"Yeah uh... it's cool," I say. What's cool? I have no idea. I don't even know how to do any of this.

"Here, can you peel these carrots?" she asks me.

"Sure," I say.

I take the peeler and grab the bag of carrots, then bring them both to the sink and start peeling away. The garbage disposal makes this easy, and I rinse off the carrots then flick the switch to turn on the garbage disposal blades once I'm done peeling them. No more mess, super clean. See, I can clean stuff, Dad?

"I really like her," I say.

Her mom turns to look at me. "Oh? Ashley?"

"Yeah. I just wanted you to know. I really like her. I don't want you getting the wrong idea here."

"Ethan, you came downstairs and told me that Ashley cockblocked you. I think I've got a pretty good idea about what's going on."

"Yeah, I guess," I say. I'm not good at this. I'm sure Ashley's great at it. But... "No," I add. "I mean, yeah, I guess, but it's different. I like that, too. The uh... physical... yeah, that. I like the physical stuff we do, but I like her as a person, too. I like the other stuff, too. It's not just um... clothesless activities..."

"Ethan, really?" my stepmom says, making a face and rolling her eyes at me.

"Look, this is kind of weird for me, alright?" I say, grinning. "I just like her. I like the cuddling, too. I like hanging out with her. And yeah, I don't know, I like the sex stuff a lot, but I like it more because she likes it, but I like everything else. I have no idea what she's talking about with her college stuff, but I like how she talks about it. She gets really excited and her nose kind of wrinkles up a little. I don't think she realizes it, but I do, and then when she's done I like to kiss her nose. She always looks at me funny, like she's wondering why I just kissed her nose, but it seems like the perfect thing to do at the time, so..."

"So you're in love with her," my stepmom says.

"Yeah," I say. To make it sound more official, I say, "Yes."

"It wasn't a question, Ethan," she says. "It was a statement."

"Oh," I say.

"You're not going to hurt her, are you?"

"I don't want to," I say. I can't say that I won't, because I don't know, but I don't want to. I don't know how to explain that one.

"You can still be yourself, Ethan," Ashley's mom says. "I know you have a reputation as being a bad boy, and you can still *be* that. You can be *her* bad boy. Does that make sense?"

"Kind of," I say.

"There's a difference between a good sort of bad and a bad bad," she says. "Girls like the good bad boys, and I think you know what that means. They don't like the bad ones, though. You can never really tell the difference between the two at first, and there's a lot more bad ones than there are good ones, but I think you're one of the good ones, Ethan. Or, you can be."

"I don't know," I say. "I fuck things up a lot."

"Sometimes," my stepmom says. "I don't think you've ever accidentally fucked something up with a girl, though. You know what you're doing, Ethan. They like you when you're with them, but then you get scared and you distance yourself from them.

You can't do that with Ashley, but I don't think I have to tell you that."

"I'm not scared," I say. It's true, because I'm not, but I don't know how to tell her the truth, either.

"Oh?" she asks.

Well, fuck, I guess I'll try! Why's she have to make this so difficult?

"I get pissed off," I say. "I don't like how guys treat the girls they're with. I know that sounds stupid, but it pisses me off to see a girl get treated like she's replaceable, and then some douchebag just treats her like shit and dumps her, breaking her heart or something. I get how it looks like I do the same thing, but I don't think it's the same."

She stops to look at me. I think she must disagree with me, maybe she's silently judging me, but then I don't think Ashley's mom would do that. Instead of doing anything else, she just smiles at me.

"I mean, I like the girls I've been with. I don't hate them. I never loved any of them, except Ashley, though. It's just... I want them to know what it's like for a guy to treat them right, and so I always swooped in and did my thing and showed them a good time. It was never supposed to be anything more than that. Then they can find a good guy who can do that shit forever. That's what I wanted to happen, but I guess maybe I went about it the wrong way."

"I can't really say you went about it the right way," Ashley's mom says with a smirk.

"Yeah, well, look, I like sex, too. I guess my intentions were never completely pure and good. I'm still a bad boy here. I've got a reputation to uphold."

"Oh, yes, of course," she says, laughing.

"I'm done, though. I promise I won't do that to Ashley. We have rules and shit. This is serious stuff. I went out with girls before, but I never really dated them. Not like a boyfriend and girlfriend thing. That's what Ashley and I are doing, though. It's legit. A real relationship."

"I'm glad to hear that," she says. "It's good to have rules and boundaries in any relationship, too."

"I don't think it's those kind of rules," I say. "It's uh... actual rules? I forget how many there are now. I think Ashley would know. Maybe we should write these down. Just not rule number one. We got rid of that one."

"What's rule number one?" Ashley's mom asks.

"That's the stepbrother with benefits one," I say without thinking. "It was only supposed to last for a week, because--"

Fuck. Did I really just say that? Ashley's mom is staring at me, unblinking.

"Stepbrother with benefits?" she asks, one eyebrow raised.

At that very moment, Ashley walks into the kitchen, freshly showered, wearing her cute shirt and shorts. She looks nice, or she did at first, but when she hears her mom say "stepbrother with benefits" she freezes, a look of horror on her face.

7 - Ashley

I DON'T REALLY KNOW what I expected to happen when my mom and Ethan's dad came home, but it definitely didn't involve finding my mom and Ethan talking about the "stepbrother with benefits" relationship he and I had agreed to try just about a week ago. In fact, if I'm being honest, that's the last thing I expected and wanted to happen.

When I walked into the kitchen, as soon as I heard my mom say that, I froze, staring at the pair of them with an open-mouthed look of shock and horror. My mom looked equally confused, and Ethan, um... he looked like Ethan? I'm not even sure if anything can phase him, and apparently having a conversation with my mom about a casual sex dalliance relationship with her daughter wasn't even on the list of discussions he thought he should be circumspect about.

"Excuse me," I say, trying to sound sweet and innocent. "What are you two talking about?"

I take it back. Yes, something can phase Ethan, and apparently it's me. "What's with the look?" Ethan asks.

"She does look scary, doesn't she?" my mom adds.

I was trying to be... nice? I think. No! I don't even want to pretend to be nice anymore. "Ethan! Seriously, you can't talk to my mom about stuff like that. That's just weird and gross and wrong."

"She told me to!" he counters.

I'm about to rant and rave at him some more, but then I realize what he just said and this changes things, now doesn't it? I glance towards my mom now. Apparently my sweet and innocent expression is really bad, because she looks at me like I'm scary. Alright, fine, I'm not even trying to be sweet and innocent anymore, but they don't have to look at me like that, do they?

"Mom," I say, whining. "What are you even doing?"

"I think there's some miscommunication going on," my mom says. "I did tell Ethan that if he needed someone to talk to about certain things, he was welcome to come to me. I didn't want him to feel left out, dear."

"I don't think that should include who I do or don't decide to have--" I stop myself before I finish that sentence, because I'm not going to admit to my mom that Ethan and I started this entire bad boy fiasco by having a "friends with benefits" type of relationship. She really doesn't have to know these things. I don't want to tell her about them in front of Ethan, at least.

"Perhaps we can make this another rule?" my mom suggests.

"Wait," I say. Wait wait wait! "Did Ethan tell you about the rules? Do you know what the rules are?"

"No?" my mom says. "I'm kind of curious, though. What are the rules?"

"Eleven is my favorite," Ethan says, because he's an idiot.

"Shut up, Ethan!" I yell at him. To my mom, I add, "Nothing, Mom. You don't have to worry about it. The rules are personal."

"Eleven?" she asks. "How many rules are there? That seems like a lot."

"Fuck if I know," Ethan says.

"Ethan, stop swearing in front of my mom," I tell him. "There's seventeen rules, too. I can't believe you can't remember that. Except one is null and void now and nine doesn't exist."

"Doesn't that mean there's only fifteen rules?" my mom asks.

"I'm not talking about the rules," I say. Then, for clarification, I add, "Not in front of Ethan."

"Wow," Ethan says, shaking his head, pretending to look sad. I don't know who he thinks he's fooling with that stupid pathetic look on his face, but it's not me. Not me at all.

"Alright," my mom says, thoughtful. "Well, how about this as a new rule or whatever you want to call it? If either of you want to talk about relationship problems with me, you can, but it has to be separate. Either just Ethan or just you, Ashley, but not the both of you together."

"I think Ethan can just talk to his dad, don't you?" I say.

"Are you crazy?" Ethan asks. "I'm not talking to my dad about this kind of stuff. That's fucked up."

"Oh, so it's alright for you to talk to *my* mom about it?" I counter. I really don't understand him.

Ethan shrugs. I turn to my mom for hopeful confirmation that I'm not crazy in feeling this way, but she just shrugs, too. Seriously? Wow. Ugh!

"Fine," I say, wrinkling my nose at the both of them. "Fine, but it's not a rule. Rules are... those are for something else. This can be, um... guideline number one."

"Got it," Ethan says. "Guideline number one. Sounds legit."

"Understood," my mother says, nodding twice. "I will adhere to your rules and guidelines."

"You're not adhering to the rules, Mom," I say, groaning at her. "Stop with the rules, please? The rules are only for us. Just for me and Ethan."

"Understood," my mom says again, nodding twice more. I wish she'd stop treating this like it's some sort of secret spy mission thing.

I guess it doesn't matter, because before I can say anything more, the phone rings. There's a phone in the kitchen right by my mom, but I can hear it ringing in the living room, and Ethan's dad's office, too. We don't really use the landline much here, but it's what I always used to call my mom from school, since she's used to it. She says it's more personal, though I really don't understand how. A phone is a phone, right?

Currently, a phone is not a phone. My mom goes to answer it, but hesitates before picking it up.

"Um, Ashley?" she says. "The caller ID says it's from Jake?"

"Motherfucker," Ethan says.

"Ethan, you can't say that in front of *my mother*," I tell him.

"What, why not--" But then it seems to dawn on him. "Oh, hey, sorry."

My mom shrugs. "It's alright, dear. No offense taken. But... Ashley, should I answer this, or...?"

As if we'd planned this, both Ethan and I say "No" at the same time.

"Well, alright," my mom says. "I just hope Ethan's father doesn't answer it, then."

"Oh, fuck," I say, forgetting myself.

Thankfully my mother didn't notice me swearing, but Ethan does. I think he would have said something, but currently we're in a pretty bad predicament, so...

Ethan's dad doesn't answer the phone and it goes to the answering machine after a couple more rings. My mom presses a button on the base to

71

listen to the message as it's recorded, which blocks it from playing on the other phones.

"Hey," Jake says into the machine. "I'm getting really sick of this, and I know something must be going on. Apparently Ashley and her boy toy are deleting these messages so that you can't hear them. This is for her mother and stepfather. I don't know if you realize this, but your daughter is having illicit sexual relations with her stepbrother, which is completely disturbing in a lot of ways. In addition to that, she's also sending him nude pictures of herself, and text messages talking about the crazy sex they're going to have. She accidentally sent me some of these, and this is how I found out. I wanted to let you know, so you can put a stop to it, but also to tell you that I'll gladly erase the evidence I have for a small fee. Please don't think of this as bribery, but as a gesture of good will. Maybe $10,000 sounds good? I'm willing to negotiate. If you get this, please call me back as soon as you can, so we can work out the details. Thanks. Oh, this is Jake, by the way. Her boyfriend from college. Sorry to be the one to tell you this."

The message stops then. Ethan and I both freeze, staring at my mother, who seems deep in thought. I'm not even sure what she's going to make of this. We haven't had a chance to talk with her about it, and I know she knows a little, but...

"Ashley," my mom says. "Why are you sending Ethan nude pictures? His bedroom is right down the hall from yours."

"Mom, are you being serious right now?" I ask her.

"She has a point, though," Ethan says, smirking at me.

My mom shrugs and lifts her eyebrows, making a face at me. "Well, it really doesn't make any sense to me, but maybe it's a thing you kids do these days, but I don't understand it at all."

"Jake is trying to blackmail you into paying him money so that he won't release pictures of me to everyone at school," I say. "I think that's a little more important, don't you?"

"Oh, is that what he's going to do with them?" my mom asks. "That's not good."

"Mom, I know it's not good."

"Pretty fucking bad if you ask me," Ethan says. "Also, he's an asshole. I should have punched him in the face again when I had the chance. What a dick."

"Did Jake come here?" my mom asks, worry knitting her brow.

"No, um..." I tell her all of it. About how the plane ticket was to go see Jake, and how he was trying to blackmail me then, too, but Ethan came and saved me, and when we got back, she'd already left with Ethan's dad for that business trip again. "That's when the first voice message came," I say. "He's left about one or two a day ever since then. We've just been deleting them."

"I'm not very happy about this," my mom says, frowning.

"I'm sorry," I say. "I... it was just something I thought would be fun, um... with Ethan, I mean. And I know it's weird, alright? I'm just--"

"What? Oh, no, not that, dear," my mom says. "I don't understand that, either, but I *understand* it, I think. It's always good to spice things up in the bedroom. Ethan's father and I do some pretty crazy things sometimes, too. I'll leave the details out."

"Um... thanks... I think?"

"What I'm not happy about is some... some asshole dick trying to hurt my daughter! My stepson, too. Who does he think he is?"

Did my mother really just call someone an asshole dick? Yes, yes she did. Ethan nods and smiles at her with his bad boy approval. Apparently he's not just rubbing off on me, but on my mother, too. This isn't good.

"We'll figure this out," my mother says. "We can talk about it together, after we talk with your father, Ethan. It's something we should do together."

"What are we talking about together?"

I jump, startled. Ethan's dad comes up behind me, putting his hand on my shoulder, smiling at all of us. I stand there, stock still, unsure what to do. Did he hear everything? Oh no...

"Who was that on the phone, by the way?" he asks.

"Wrong number," my mother says, smiling sweetly and innocently. She's much better at this than I am. "We were just talking about where we should go for dinner. Wouldn't it be nice to eat out as a family on our first night back, with all of us together?"

"Sounds great," my stepfather says. "I'm tired of all that business junk we had to deal with. Work work work. Hey, we can talk about the camping trip, too. I know it's short notice, but how about we leave tomorrow? I don't want anyone to interrupt us and try to tell me I need to come back to work for something, so the sooner the better. Would love to have some quality time with the family. What does everyone think?"

It's unanimous, we all agree. That seems to settle it, and we start to move out of the kitchen, the chopped vegetables for the snack my mom was making all but forgotten. It's probably for the best, because if she mentioned it, Ethan's dad would say we could hang around and then go to dinner later, but I really need to get out of the house right now. I need to forget about Jake, and about what Ethan and my mom were talking about, and just all of it.

I don't know what I expected to happen, and I thought I could stay with Ethan on our own little imaginary island, but apparently not. I know my mom seems alright with it, but...

"Oh, Ashley," Ethan's dad says. "I didn't have a chance to ask you before, but how was your visit with your friend? Did you have a good time?"

Mia Clark

8 - Ethan

YOU EVER JUST FIND YOURSELF hanging around, doing your own thing, and then someone says something completely stupid? And it's not just stupid, but it's probably the worst thing anyone could ever say at that exact moment, which makes you wonder if it's coincidence or something else?

I know my dad couldn't possibly know that what he just said was horrible, but uh... yeah, Dad, what you just said was horrible.

I kind of want to say something to him, but I can't. I kind of want to go give Ashley a hug just to tell her that it's alright and my dad's not actually a huge prick, but I can't do that, either. The only thing I can do is stand there and watch and hope we get the fuck out of the house sooner rather than later.

Ashley laughs it off, though the look in her eyes says she's anything but amused right now. She doesn't look mad or anything, just hurt and sad. It's a hard look to really narrow down into an actual emotion, but her eyes just kind of droop a little, her expression goes slightly blank, even if she tries to hide it with a smile. It's easy for me to tell, but I doubt my dad notices.

"I ended up coming home early," she says. "There were some unforeseen circumstances."

"Ah," my dad says, nodding. "I understand. Things happen. I hope it was nothing too serious?"

Pretty serious, I think. Serious enough that I had to fly after her and kick her ex-boyfriend's ass. Oh well, what can you do? I'd do it again if I had to.

Ashley shrugs it off and makes a little sound of indifference, sort of between a grunt and a mumble. That seems good enough for my dad. We all head out to get our shoes and junk, which means Ashley and I end up going upstairs together. She quietly heads to her end of the hallway while I'm supposed to be going to mine and my room, but, nah, I've got something else in mind.

I sneak along after her while she steps down the hall, and then I grab her waist and stop her. She stiffens, then lets out a squeak, but I'm not even done with this girl yet. I take a step close, swoop down, then pick her up in my arms. This isn't something soft and gentle, it's intimate as fuck. I'm holding her, cradled, her back tight in one of my arms, and her legs caught in my other. I squeeze her close to me and carry her the rest of the way down the hall to her room.

"Hey," I say.

"Hi," she says, smiling at me. Her arms reach up and she wraps them around my neck, pulling herself even closer to me.

"Sorry about that," I tell her. "It's cool, alright? We'll figure this out, and I'll go kick that prick's ass again if I have to. I'm sure my dad won't mind."

"It was just a shock," she says. "I didn't think about Jake calling when our parents were back, and then he did, and then your dad said that, and--"

Blah blah blah. You know how I fix things like this? Actually, I have no fucking clue, because I usually don't deal with this shit, but how I'm going to deal with it now is to kiss the fuck out of this gorgeous fucking princess I've got trapped in my arms. I press my lips against hers and grin at the startled look on her face. What, you think I won't kiss you, Ashley? I'll kiss you whenever I want, baby girl...

She kisses me back after a second, and then I move to the bed with her, sitting us both down. She whimpers and complains for a second, mumbling at me, but I am pretty fucking sure that I could have a lot of sex with her right now if I wanted. Lock the door, ignore my dad and her mom if they come calling after us, and just spend the entire night in bed with her, with my cock buried inside her.

I'm not going to do that, but I'm pretty sure I could, that's all.

Meek and unbelievable, she says, "Ethan, we can't do this. Have sex, I mean. Not right now."

"Who said anything about having sex?" I ask her.

She gives me a look. It's that look that says she totally knows I was thinking about having sex with her.

"Listen, Princess," I tell her, grinning. "I know what's up. You don't have to tell me. Just don't go lying to me. You'd love it if I ripped your shorts off and shoved my face between your thighs right now."

"Well, I would like that..." she says, biting her bottom lip. Fuck, that's cute.

"I've been thinking," I say.

"Oh, you have?" she asks, smirking at me. "*You?* Ethan Colton? I didn't know you could think. Not with something besides this, at least." *This* being my cock, which she reaches down to squeeze through my pants.

"Don't make this worse for yourself, Princess," I say, smirking right back at her. "What I've been thinking is I've heard a lot of good things about something you might know as anticipation, and I thought we could put it into practice starting tonight."

"Anticipation?" she asks, giving me a silly smile. "What's that?"

"I've got to tell Little Miss Perfect Grades the definition of anticipation?" I ask. "Holy fuck, the world's coming to an end."

"Shut up," she says. "I know what anticipation means! I didn't think you did. Have you ever waited for anything in your entire life?"

"Yeah," I say. "I did. I've waited for you since the second grade."

I didn't even realize what I said until after I said it, but uh... fuck, did I just say that? Yeah, I guess I did. She stares at me, just looks into my eyes, and I feel like there's a crazy strong connection there. I've felt like this ever since we started this crazy relationship a crazy week ago, but this is even more crazy somehow.

"Second grade?" she asks me. "Really?"

"Yeah, I don't know. That was a dumb thing to say."

"No!" she says, strong. "No, I liked it. It was really sweet, Ethan. If you meant it, it was."

Did I mean it? I don't know. Fuck. This question is harder than anything I've had to answer before, and some of those questions on school tests are pretty fucking difficult. How do I pass this relationship exam? I have no idea.

"I thought you were cool back then," I say. "I mean, I didn't love you or anything, but I thought you were cool and I liked hanging out with you."

"You were kind of a jerk to me, though," she counters.

"Yeah, well... I'm kind of a jerk to everyone."

My sweetness points are being blown completely out the window right about now, aren't they? I need to Google how to be in a relationship or something, because this shit is difficult as fuck.

"You can just tell me," she says. "I know this is weird for you, but it's weird for me, too, and you can just tell me what you think and what you're thinking. How about we make that rule number eighteen?"

"We're still doing the rules?" I ask her with a grin.

"Yup!" she says.

"Alright, rule number eighteen. What is it?"

"We have to be open with one another," she says. "It's different from rule number seven, which is the one about lying, though. This is just about telling each other how we feel, and we have to be open with one another."

"I can do that," I say.

"Alright, good," she says. "Do it."

Open with each other? How do I feel right now? Uh... I don't know, hold on, give me a second to think about this.

"First off," I say. "I want to rip off your shorts and shove my face between your thighs."

"That's not what I meant!" she says, slapping my shoulder, playful.

"Fuck," I say, laughing. "I thought I was good at this for a second."

"Tell me the second grade thing!" she shrieks and tries to tickle me. Oh, you want to play that game?

I toss her onto the bed and out of my lap, then I wrap my fingers around her waist and tickle her. She laughs and squeaks and wriggles, but I don't let her go. I don't want to ever let her go. I want to see her laughing forever. I always want to see her smile and be happy.

I stop tickling her after she begs and pleads with me. I lay on my back on the bed next to her and take in a deep breath, sighing.

"When I first met you I thought you were crazy," I tell her. "You were weird and you didn't make sense to me at all. You were kind of like an alien in my mind, but I was young so what the fuck do I know?"

She snorts at me and makes a face, wrinkling her nose and pursing her lips.

"You made me think about things I've never thought about before, though," I add. "I remember when we were swinging, and I was trying to go as high as I could, because I thought that's what you were supposed to do on swings, but you asked me why I was doing that. You said it was too much, and it wasn't as fun. I thought you were crazy, Princess, but then I slowed down, and I let myself just enjoy the ride. I let myself experience something I'd never even considered before, and it was amazing. That's how I felt about you then, and that's how I feel about you now."

Her snort, funny face, wrinkled up nose, pursed lips... they vanish into what can only be described as a puppy dog face. It's that face that girls get when they're looking at a puppy dog that's adorable as fuck and they just want to squeeze it. Apparently I'm the puppy dog right now, because that's exactly what she does. She hops on top of me and squeezes me tight, then kisses my face.

"You really are sweet when you want to be," she says. "Also, I love you."

"*Also?*" I ask, laughing. "Yeah, yeah, I love you, too, Princess."

"I'm going to do so many dirty things to you later, Ethan Colton," she says, giving me a seductive and sultry look. "How's that for anticipation?"

"Whoa, changing gears there kind of fast, aren't you?"

"Nope!" she says, shaking her head quick. "I like you when you're a bad boy, but I love you when you're sweet. It makes me want to be extra naughty and dirty..."

I don't even know how to begin to comprehend that. She's seriously crazy. I thought she was crazy when we were in second grade, and I think she's extra crazy now, but she's my crazy, and I kind of like it. Also, you think I can pass up this gorgeous as fuck girl in my lap saying she wants to be extra naughty and dirty with me? No fucking chance in hell.

"Go put your shoes on," I tell her. "We've got to go to dinner."

I laugh and toss her off of me and back onto her bed. She pouts and stares after me as I head to her door, to the hallway, to my room.

"You better not eat too much for dinner," she says just as I pass the precipice from her room to the hallway. "I've got dessert for you later."

I shouldn't do this. I know it, I really fucking know it, and I shouldn't do it, but I turn around to make some snide retort or something, except she kills me. I'm dead. Mortally wounded on this battlefield of uh... I don't know? Lust or love or relationships or something.

Ashley lays on the bed, rubbing her crotch. She's got shorts on, but they're pretty short, especially since she's laying down and they're partly hiked up her thigh. I can see the barest inkling of her panties through the bottom of her shorts, and her slow, languorous strokes aren't helping all that much. To make matters worse, she has her hand up her shirt, squeezing one of her breasts, and her eyes are closed. She licks her lips and moans.

Oh yeah? Two can play at that game, Princess. Don't you even fucking try to win this.

"Hey, Mom!" I say loudly. "You didn't have to come up here. We'll be down in a second."

Ashley panics and pulls her hand out from under her shirt and away from her shorts-covered sex in a rush to sit up and look like she was doing anything but trying to lure me into temptation. Not that she has to do anything to do that, but, you know. She's pretty good at it for a good girl. Who knew?

I should probably mention that her mom isn't anywhere nearby. I was just being a jerk.

When she realizes this, she glares at me. "Seriously, Ethan?" she asks, trying not to laugh. "You're a huge jerk!"

"Seriously, Ashley?" I counter, grinning. "Tell me something I don't know."

What, you thought that just because we were dating now I'd stop teasing her? Uh... nah, not ever going to happen. Teasing Ashley is just about my favorite thing to do in the world. Sorry, second favorite. Maybe third, now that I think about it. Cuddling and fucking are pretty amazing, to be honest.

Heart-to-heart talks are pretty great, too. Maybe teasing her is my fourth favorite thing. I'll figure it out later.

A NOTE FROM MIA

THERE'S MORE ETHAN AND ASHLEY! YAY!

Initially, I'd only planned on the writing and releasing the original stories. I wasn't sure how they'd be received, and I didn't want to get too far ahead of myself just in case. But... there's been an overwhelming response, so here they are again, and I hope you're enjoying their return!

This is what I'm calling the "Second Season" of Ethan and Ashley, which I think makes sense. Like a TV show, right? Unfortunately I didn't have all of it written yet, so I can't publish them all at once, but everyone was asking for more, so I wanted to get more as soon as I could. That kind of means there's might be a little bit of a wait in between books, but I promise I'll make it as painless as possible.

My goal is to publish a new book in this season every two weeks, which follows about how long it took me to originally write the first Stepbrother With Benefits books. I'm also aiming for six books for this season. The season will take place throughout the camping trip, and will mostly involve Ashley and Ethan's relationship evolving while they try to figure out how to tell Ethan's dad, and some other crazy things happening. It should be fun, and I've got it all plotted out, but I've just got to write it first.

I hope you've liked this first episode of the season, and I hope you'll keep an eye out for the next one. It should be coming around the June 7th or so, and I'm really looking forward to it!

If you did like this new beginning, I'd love if you rated and reviewed it on Amazon, too. It helps a lot and I appreciate it so much!

Thank you for sticking around with me for all of the fun and steaminess of Ethan and Ashley's story, and I can't wait to bring you more. Don't forget to sign up for my VIP readers list and follow me on Facebook so you can get updates and sneak peeks and firsthand knowledge of when my new releases are out!

Bye!

$\sim$MIA

ABOUT THE AUTHOR

Mia likes to have fun in all aspects of her life. Whether she's out enjoying the beautiful weather or spending time at home reading a book, a smile is never far from her face. She's prone to randomly laughing at nothing in particular except for whatever idea amuses her at any given moment.

Sometimes you just need to enjoy life, right?

She loves to read, dance, and explore outdoors. Chamomile tea and bubble baths are two of her favorite things. Flowers are especially nice, and she could get lost in a garden if it's big enough and no one's around to remind her that there are other things to do.

She lives in New Hampshire, where the weather is beautiful and the autumn colors are amazing.

Manufactured by Amazon.ca
Bolton, ON